All the Places to Love

BY PATRICIA MacLACHLAN

PAINTINGS BY MIKE WIMMER

HarperCollins*Publishers*

All the Places to Love

Text copyright © 1994 by Patricia MacLachlan

Illustrations copyright © 1994 by Mike Wimmer

Printed in the U.S.A. All rights reserved.

Library of Congress Cataloging-in-Publication Data

MacLachlan, Patricia.

   All the places to love / by Patricia MacLachlan ; paintings by Mike Wimmer.

     p.   cm.

   Summary: A young boy describes the favorite places that he shares with his family on his grandparents' farm and in the nearby countryside.

   ISBN 0-06-021098-2. — ISBN 0-06-021099-0 (lib. bdg.)

   [1. Farms—Fiction.   2. Country life—Fiction.]   I. Wimmer, Mike, ill.   II. Title.

PZ7.M2225Al   1994   92-794

[E]—dc20   CIP

                                                             AC

Typography by Al Cetta

Title lettering by Anton Kimball

5 6 7 8 9 10

❖

This is for Bill Morris

—with love

P. M.

Dedicated to my grandparents,

Jace and Goldie Hambrick,

for their sixty-four years of marriage

which serve as the mortar

that binds my family together.

M. W.

On the day I was born

My grandmother wrapped me in a blanket

made from the wool of her sheep.

She held me up in the open window

So that what I heard first was the wind.

What I saw first were all the places to love:

The valley,

The river falling down over rocks,

The hilltop where the blueberries grew.

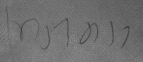

My grandfather was painting the barn,

And when he saw me he cried.

He carved my name —ELI—

On a rafter beside his name

And Grandmother's name

And the names of my papa and mama.

Mama carried me on her shoulders before I could walk,

Through the meadows and hay fields.

The cows watched us and the sheep scattered;

The dogs ran ahead, looking back with sly smiles.

When the grass was high

Only their tails showed.

When I was older, Papa and I plowed the fields.

Where else is soil so sweet? he said.

Once Papa and I lay down in the field, holding hands,

And the birds surrounded us:

Raucous black grackles, redwings,

Crows in the dirt that swaggered like pirates.

When we left, Papa put a handful of dirt in his pocket.

I did too.

My grandmother loved the river best

   of all the places to love.

That sound, like a whisper, she said;

Gathering in pools

Where trout flashed like jewels in the sunlight.

Grandmother sailed little bark boats downriver to me

With messages.

I Love You Eli, one said.

We jumped from rock to rock to rock,

Across the river to where the woods began,

Where bunchberry grew under the pine-needle path

And trillium bloomed.

Under the beech tree was a soft, rounded bed

where a deer had slept.

The bed was warm when I touched it.

When spring rains came and the meadow turned to marsh,

Cattails stood like guards, and killdeers called.

Ducks nested by marsh marigolds,

And the old turtle—his shell all worn—

No matter how slow,

Still surprised me.

Sometimes we climbed to the place Mama loved best,

With our blueberry buckets and a chair for my grandmother:

To the blueberry barren where no trees grew—

The sky an arm's length away;

Where marsh hawks skimmed over the land,

And bears came to eat fruit,

And wild turkeys left footprints for us to find,

Like messages.

Where else, said my mama, *can I see the sun rise on one side*

And the sun set on the other?

My grandfather's barn is sweet-smelling

  and dark and cool;

Leather harnesses hang like paintings against old wood;

And hay dust floats like gold in the air.

Grandfather once lived in the city,

And once he lived by the sea;

But the barn is the place he loves most.

Where else, he says, *can the soft sound of cows chewing*

Make all the difference in the world?

Today we wait, him sitting on a wooden-slat chair

And me on the hay,

Until, much later, my grandmother holds up a small bundle
  in the open window,

Wrapped in a blanket made from the wool of her sheep,

And my grandfather cries.

Together

We carve the name SYLVIE in the rafter

Beside the names of Grandfather and Grandmother,

And my mama and papa,

And me.

My sister is born.

Someday I might live in the city.

Someday I might live by the sea.

But soon I will carry Sylvie on my shoulders

   through the fields;

I will send her messages downriver in small boats;

And I will watch her at the top of the hill,

Trying to touch the sky.

I will show her my favorite place, the marsh,

Where ducklings follow their mother

Like tiny tumbles of leaves.

All the places to love are here, I'll tell her,

no matter where you may live.

Where else, I will say, *does an old turtle crossing the path*

Make all the difference in the world?